This book belongs to:

. . . .

. . . .

Editor: Lucy Cuthew
Designer: Cathy Tincknell
Series Editor: Ruth Symons
Editorial Director: Victoria Garrard
Art Director: Laura Roberts-Jensen

Copyright © QED Publishing 2014
First published in the UK in 2014 by QED Publishing
A Quarto Group company
The Old Brewery
6 Blundell Street
London N7 9BH
www.qed-publishing.co.uk

A catalogue record for this book is available from the British Library.

ISBN 978 1 78171 645 8

Printed in China

Eat Your Greens, Goldilocks

Written by **Steve Smallman**

Illustrated by **Bruno Robert**

QED Publishing

O nce upon a time there was a little girl called Goldilocks. She had big blue eyes, curly, golden hair... and a very bad temper!

"Eat your cereal," said her mum.

"**Yuck!**" shouted Goldilocks. She would NEVER eat anything healthy.

"Just try it," begged her dad.

"NO!" screamed Goldilocks.
"I WANT JELLY AND
ICE CREAM AND
I WANT THEM
NOW!"

But she didn't get them,
so she got up and ran away!

Goldilocks ran through the forest.
Before long, she was lost and
tired and her tummy was rumbling.

She wished she'd eaten breakfast.

Then she smelled
something yummy!

She followed her nose to a little cottage.
No one was home, so she went inside.

"Phew, I need a sit down!"
said Goldilocks.

First she sat on a big chair...

"OUCH! Too hard!"
she said.

Then she sat on a
middle-sized chair...

"OOH! Too soft!"
she said.

Then she sat on a little chair...

"Ahh, just right," she said, then,

"EEEEEK!" as the
little chair fell to pieces.

She landed,

BUMP,

on the floor.

Sitting up, she smelled
the yummy smell again.
It was coming from the
next room...

On the table were three bowls of porridge.

"Not poopy gloopy porridge!" moaned Goldilocks.

But her tummy grumbled so loudly that she decided to try it.

First she tried the big bowl...

"Ouch! Too hot!"

she said and threw it
on the floor.

Then she tried the
middle-sized bowl...

"Bleugh! Too cold!"

she said and threw it
at the wall.

Then she tried the
little bowl...

"Yummy! Just right!"

she cried, and she
gobbled it all up!

By now Goldilocks felt sleepy, so she crept upstairs and found the bedroom.

First she tried the big bed...

"OUCH! Too hard!"

she said.

Then she tried the
middle-sized bed...

Then she tried the little bed...

"OOH!
Too soft!"

she said.

"Ahhh, just
right!"

she sighed.

And she fell
fast asleep.

While Goldilocks slept,
three bears came in:
big **Daddy Bear**,
middle-sized Mummy Bear
and little Baby Bear.

They found Baby Bear's broken chair,
porridge all over the kitchen and
Baby Bear's porridge... all gone!

Then they saw muddy
footprints leading up
the stairs...

"Somebody's been sleeping in my bed!"
said Daddy Bear.

"Somebody's been
sleeping in my bed!"
said Mummy Bear.

"Somebody's STILL
sleeping in my bed!"
said Baby Bear. "Look!"

"WHO ARE YOU
AND WHAT HAVE
YOU DONE TO
OUR HOUSE?"
roared Daddy Bear.

Goldilocks woke up.

"I... I'm Goldilocks and I'm sorry!" she cried.

"You'd better come
to the kitchen,"
growled Daddy Bear.

"They're going to eat me!"
thought Goldilocks.

First Daddy Bear made Goldilocks mend the chair.

"Time for a snack," said Mummy Bear.

"*They're going to eat me!*"
thought Goldilocks.

But Mummy Bear handed
Goldilocks a banana and
a glass of milk.

Goldilocks ate the banana
and drank the milk.

"Yummy!"

Then Mummy Bear made Goldilocks clean up the porridge.

"Time for lunch!" said Daddy Bear.

"*They're going to eat me!*" thought Goldilocks.

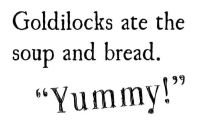

But Daddy Bear handed her a bowl of soup and a slice of bread.

Goldilocks ate the soup and bread.

"Yummy!"

When Goldilocks had washed the stairs and made the beds, Daddy Bear said, "Time for dinner!"

"Please don't eat me!" cried Goldilocks.

"We don't want to eat you!" said Daddy Bear. "We only eat nice, healthy food."

Mummy Bear put a chicken casserole and
a bowl of steaming vegetables on the table.

Goldilocks was so hungry after all the
work that she helped herself to a huge
portion and ate it all up!

"SCRUMMY!"

After dinner, the bears walked Goldilocks home. On the way they picked some blackberries.

"These would be lovely with jelly and ice cream!" Baby Bear said.

"You eat jelly and ice cream?"
gasped Goldilocks in surprise.

"Of course, but only as a treat!" said Baby Bear.
"Never for breakfast!"

Next steps

Show the children the cover again. When they first saw it, did they think that they already knew this story? How is this story different from the traditional story? Which bits are the same?

Goldilocks was very naughty while inside the three bears' cottage. What did she do that was wrong? When Daddy Bear woke Goldilocks up, how was he feeling? Was it fair that the bears made Goldilocks do all that hard work, cleaning and mending?

What did Goldilocks think that the bears were going to do with her? What did they actually do?

Did Goldilocks think the food the bears gave her was going to be nice? Ask the children if they have ever thought something was going to taste yucky, and it was actually yummy.

Ask the children to draw their favourite food. Do they think this food is healthy, or should it just be eaten as a treat? Why is it important to eat healthy food?